My Friend Angry

By Amy Krohn
Illustrated by Brian Barber

For my kids and co-creators: Hannah, Jennie, John, and Daniel. —AK

For my mom and dad, who have always been supportive of the artsy things. —BB

My Friend Angry © copyright 2021 by Amy Krohn. All rights reserved. No part of this book may be reproduced in any form whatsoever, especially cell division, by photography or xerography or by any other means, medians, or modes, by broadcast or transmission, manual or otherwise, by translation into any kind of language, especially Pig Latin, nor by recording electronically or otherwise, without permission in writing from the author or designated humpback whale; except by a reviewer, who may quote brief passages in critical articles or reviews.

Edited by Lily Coyle
Illustrated by Brian Barber
Production editor: Hanna Kjeldbjerg
Author photo by: VIVID Photography Studio

ISBN 13: 978-1-64343-861-0
Library of Congress Catalog Number: 2020912713
Printed in the United States of America
First Printing: 2020
25 24 23 22 21   5 4 3 2 1

Book design and typesetting by Brian Barber.

 Beaver's Pond Press
939 Seventh Street West
Saint Paul, MN 55102
(952) 829-8818
www.beaverspondpress.com

 MIX
Paper from responsible sources
FSC® C008080

To order, visit www.amyjkrohn.com. Reseller discounts available.

Contact Amy Krohn at www.amyjkrohn.com for school visits, speaking engagements, group coaching events, and interviews.

It's okay to be Angry.
Don't fight it,
Don't hate it,
Don't make it go.
Love it instead,
Let it be at Home.

One day
Vanessa was angry.
Really, REALLY angry.
Her throat was tangly tight.
Her face was flushed and fierce.
Her stomach was in
Gnarled, naggy knots.

Her stormy inside was going to burst
Right through her skin,
Right through the walls of her house.

So she ran
Out the back door,
Down the steps,

Into the yard,
And across the park—
Fast,

A raging bull
With sharp horns
And pounding hooves.

At the big corner tree, she stopped,
With boiling and blazing breath.
"I FEEL ANGRY!" she screamed to the air.

No one answered.

"REALLY, REALLY ANGRY!"
She screamed to the whole world.
She looked around.

No one was there.
No one to listen to all her anger.
Except her.

She huffed
And slumped down by the tree.
All of a sudden . . .

Angry was a
Snippy, snaggy,

Surly, sulky,

Scurvy, scorch of. . .

Well, anger!

Vanessa was not in the mood for this. "Go away," she grouched.

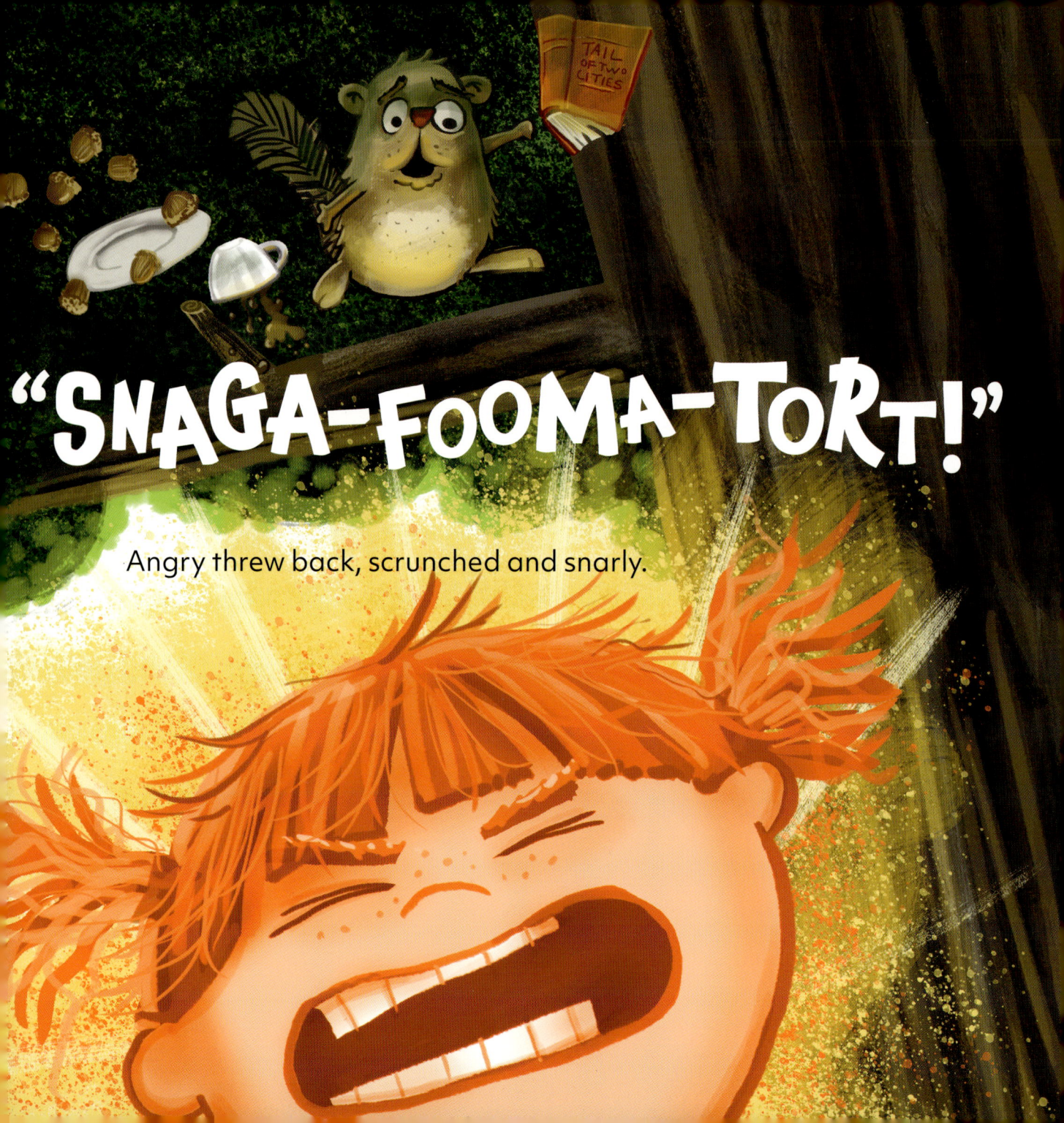

Angry started shouting
And spinning like a
Loud little lava tornado.
It was SO annoying.
Vanessa slammed her eyes shut
And covered her ears.
"Stop!" she growled.

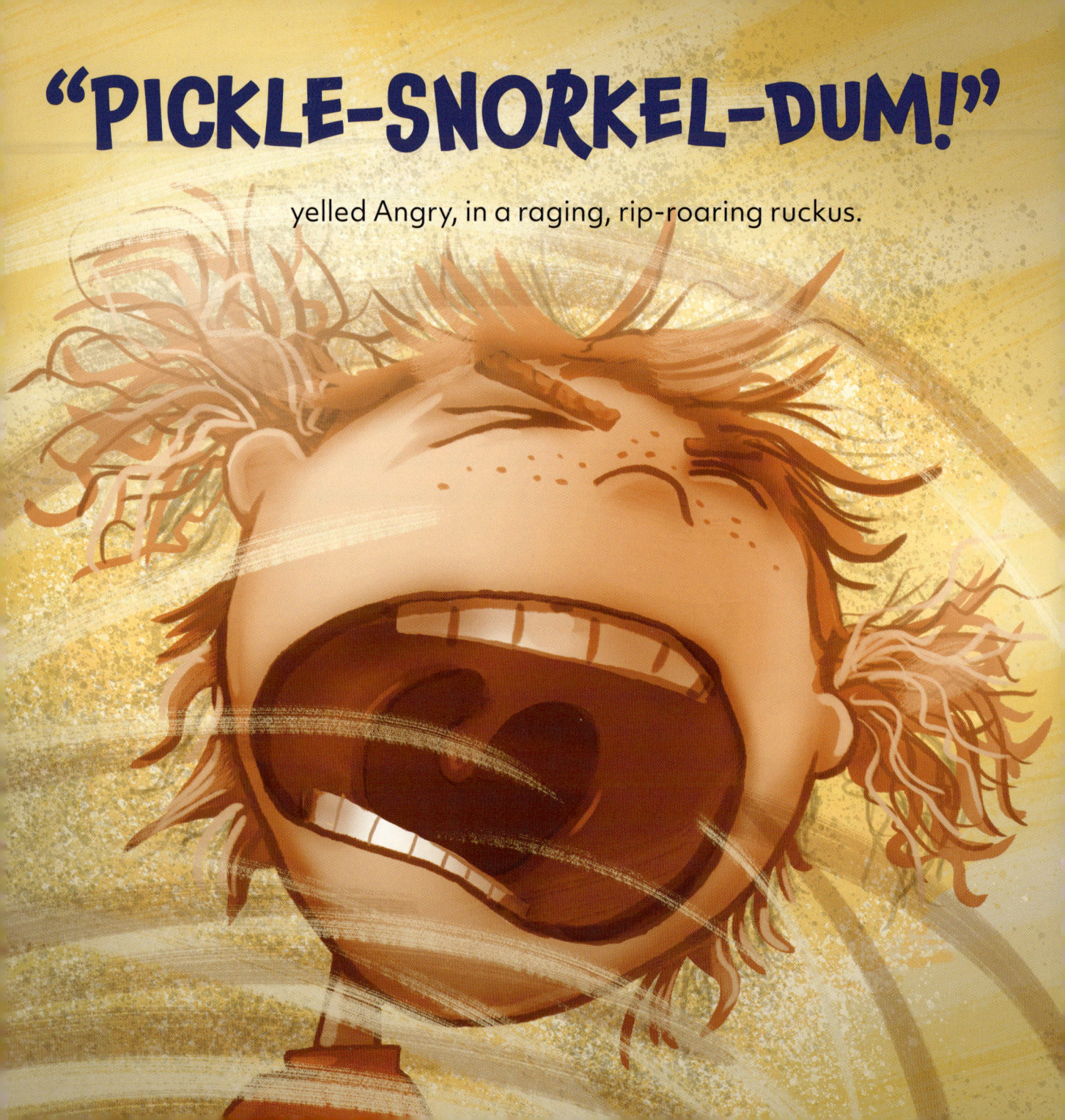

"PICKLE-SNORKEL-DUM!"

yelled Angry, in a raging, rip-roaring ruckus.

That was it.
Vanessa had enough.
She jumped to her feet.

"KNOCK IT OFF!" she shouted.

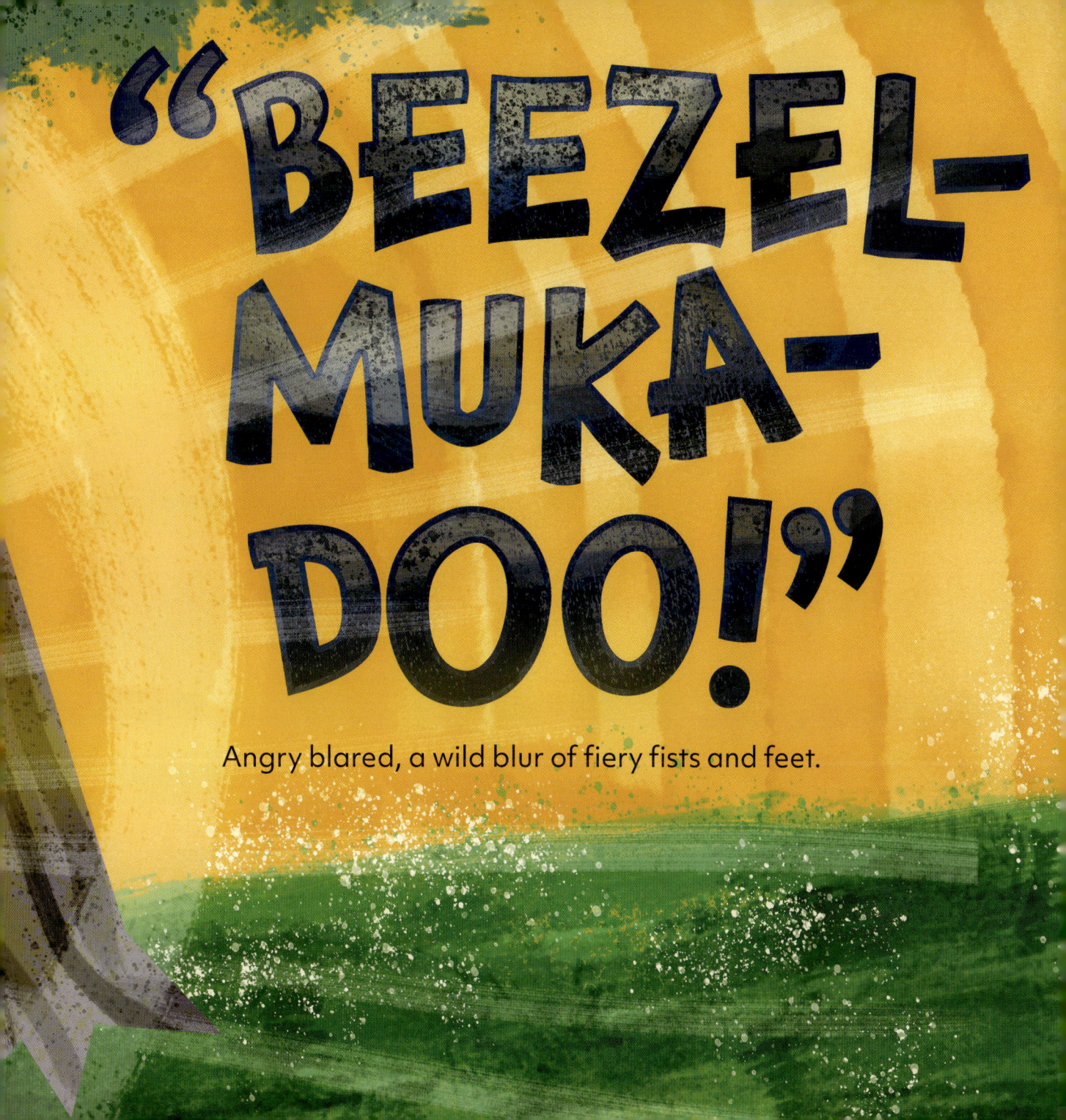

Vanessa sighed.
This was not working.
"Fine," she said.
"What do you want?"

With that, Angry suddenly stopped.
And stood there.
Still. Quiet.
Vanessa took a deep breath,
Reached out a hand,
And gently touched her Angry.
Angry's shoulders slumped.
Angry's head drooped.
Angry sagged to the ground.
Drippy droppy tears started to fall.

Vanessa sat down with her Angry.
And they just sat.
Letting Angry be Angry.
And Vanessa be Vanessa.
Pretty soon, Angry started to talk.
Angry told Vanessa what it's like
To be
Her Angry.

Angry always starts out small:
Shifty shoulders,
Tight tummy,
Irritated eyebrows.

But if Vanessa doesn't
Feel her Angry
Or ignores her Angry?
Well then.
Angry has to take
Drastic measures
Like shouting and stomping
And blaming.

It doesn't feel good.
It's not supposed to feel good.
But that's why no one likes Angry.
No one wants Angry.
Angry is told to "Stop!"
Or "Go away!"

Vanessa took a deep breath.
Angry was just trying
To get her attention.
Angry was only here
To be Seen
And Loved.

"Thanks for telling me," she said.
"It's okay. You can stay with me.
You are MY Angry."

Vanessa got up slowly,
Brushed off her knees,
Looked around,
And smiled to herself.

Do YOU feel angry sometimes?

Does your Angry ever feel really **BIG**? Even **BEEZEL-MUCKA-DOO** big?

It's okay—mine does too! No matter how big our Angry gets, feelings are simply energy, and energy can easily be moved. Vanessa became friends with her Angry, and you can be friends with your Angry too! Here's how:

1 Slow Down. Vanessa and Angry were stuck in a struggle until Vanessa slowed down. Then Angry could slow down too.

2 Feel. Go inside your body and feel the energy of Angry. How does it feel? Where does it live in your body? What is its size, shape, and color? What are YOUR words for your Angry?

3 Stay. We may want to get away from our Angry because it doesn't feel "good." Stay with your Angry! Our feelings are OUR feelings—they belong to us. Feeling is an inside job, so acting out our Angry is not staying. Doing something just to feel better is ignoring Angry. Just stay. It's okay to cry—tears are excellent energy movers. (Like mini mighty Mississippi Rivers!) Asking a trusted adult or friend to stay with you is okay too.

4 Breathe. Take a deep breath. Or two. Or twenty. Move air—make your very own giant gusts of wind! Breathing is ALL ABOUT moving energy. When Angry gets big, deep breaths can help us stay.

5 Make It Okay. Say "It's okay, Angry, I've got you!" When we accept and love our Angry as a friend, just the way it is, Angry can easily shift . . . all by itself.

Have fun playing with your new friend Angry!

All my love, *Amy*

I LOVE hearing from you! Send me artwork of your friend Angry, tell me about what your Angry is like, or what you imagine Vanessa will do next. Ask an adult to help you visit www.amyjkrohn.com to send a picture or write a letter. There are lots of fun activities to check out as well. Let's PLAY!

Special Note to Adults: *If you have kids in your life experiencing anger, follow the steps above for yourself first. Every time. We cannot "help" anyone—even children—with anger. Our subconscious feelings create our reality, so if we see anger in someone else, it is a mirror for OUR anger asking to be seen by US. When we own and love our feelings, everyone in our lives receives an immediate permission slip to do the same. Do your inner work and watch your whole world transform!*